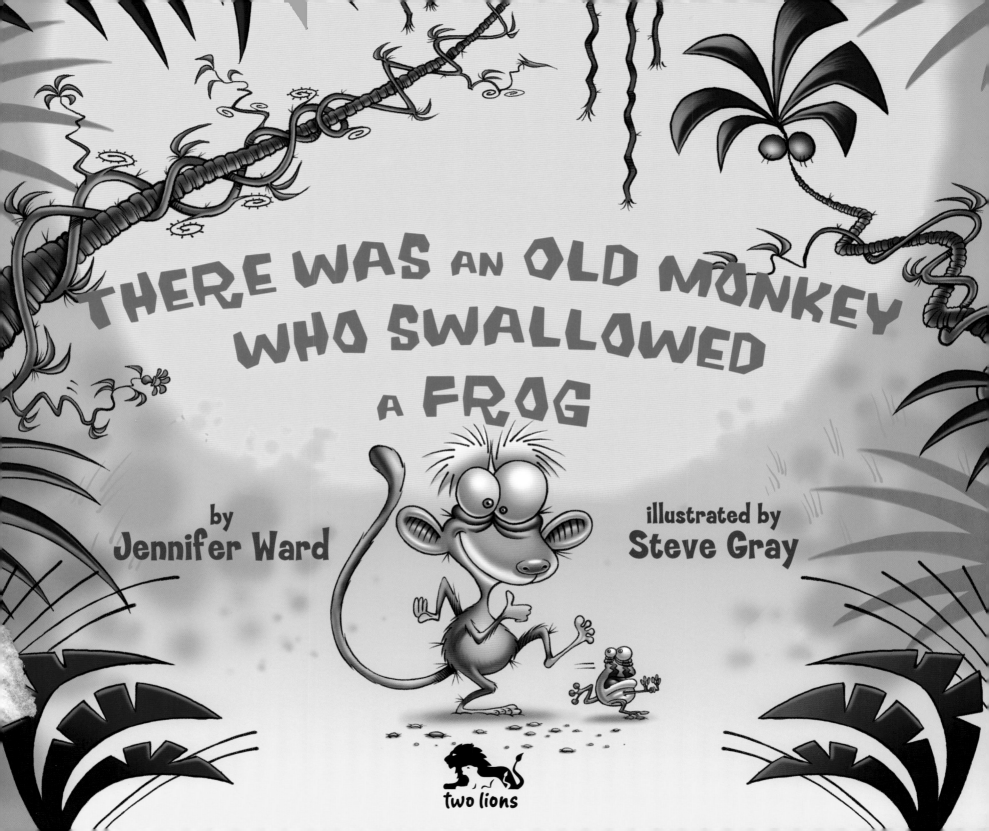

THERE WAS AN OLD MONKEY WHO SWALLOWED A FROG

by
Jennifer Ward

illustrated by
Steve Gray

two lions

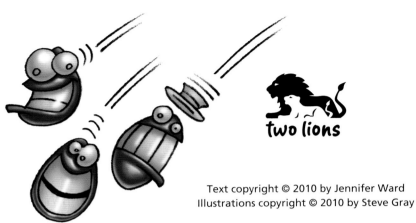

Text copyright © 2010 by Jennifer Ward
Illustrations copyright © 2010 by Steve Gray

All rights reserved
Amazon Publishing
Attn: Amazon Children's Publishing
P.O. Box 400818, Las Vegas, NV 89140
www.amazon.com/amazonchildrenspublishing

Library of Congress Cataloging-in-Publication Data
Ward, Jennifer, 1963-
There was an old monkey who swallowed a frog /
by Jennifer Ward ; illustrated by Steve Gray. — 1st ed.
    p. cm.
  Summary: Set in the jungle, this variation on the tra-
ditional, cumulative rhyme looks at the consequences
of a monkey's strange diet.
  ISBN 978-0-7614-5580-6
  1. Folk songs, English—England—Texts. [1. Folk
songs—England. 2. Songs. 3. Nonsense verses.]
I. Gray, Steve, 1950- ill. II. Little old lady who swallowed
a fly. III. Title.
PZ8.3.W2135Thk 2010
782.42—dc22
[E]
                                        2009005925

The illustrations are rendered in digital media.
Book design by Vera Soki
Editor: Marilyn Mark

Printed in China
First edition
1 3 5 6 4 2

For Charlie, monkey extraordinaire   —J.W.

To CJ . . . Guess what? I'm YOUR biggest fan!   —S.G.

There was
an old monkey . . .

who
swallowed
a frog.

I don't know why he
swallowed the frog.

What a hog!

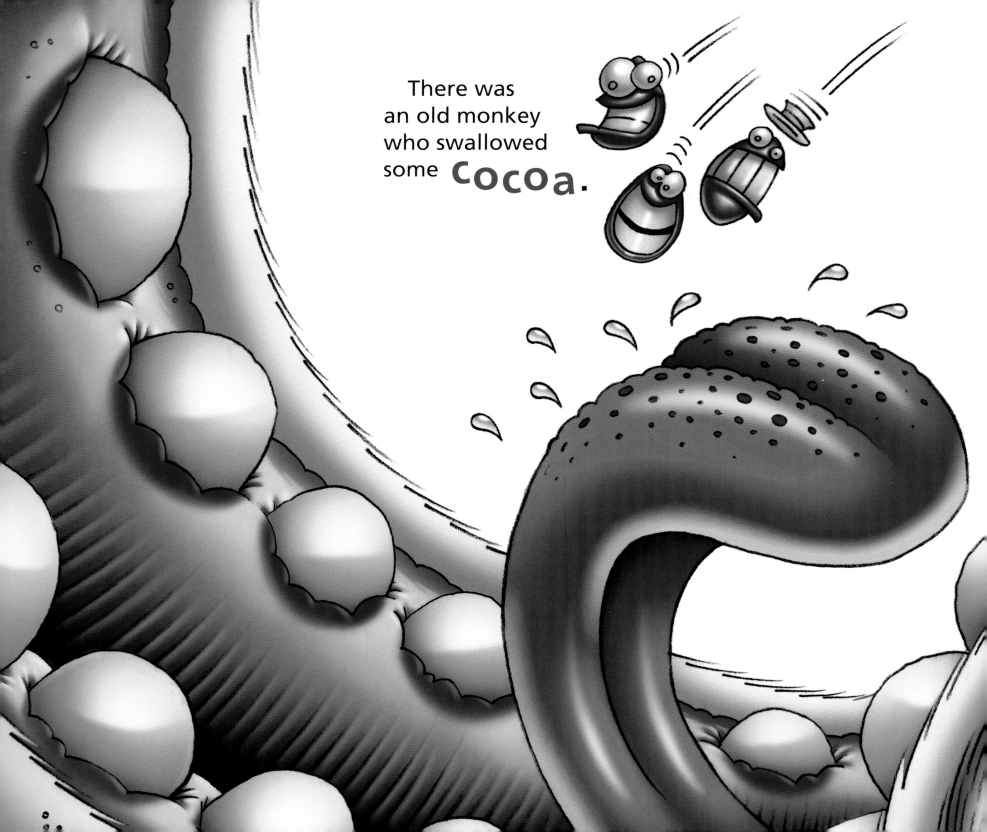

There was an old monkey who swallowed some **Cocoa**.

It made him act loco,
that chocolaty cocoa!

He swallowed the cocoa
to sweeten the frog.
I don't know why he
swallowed the frog.

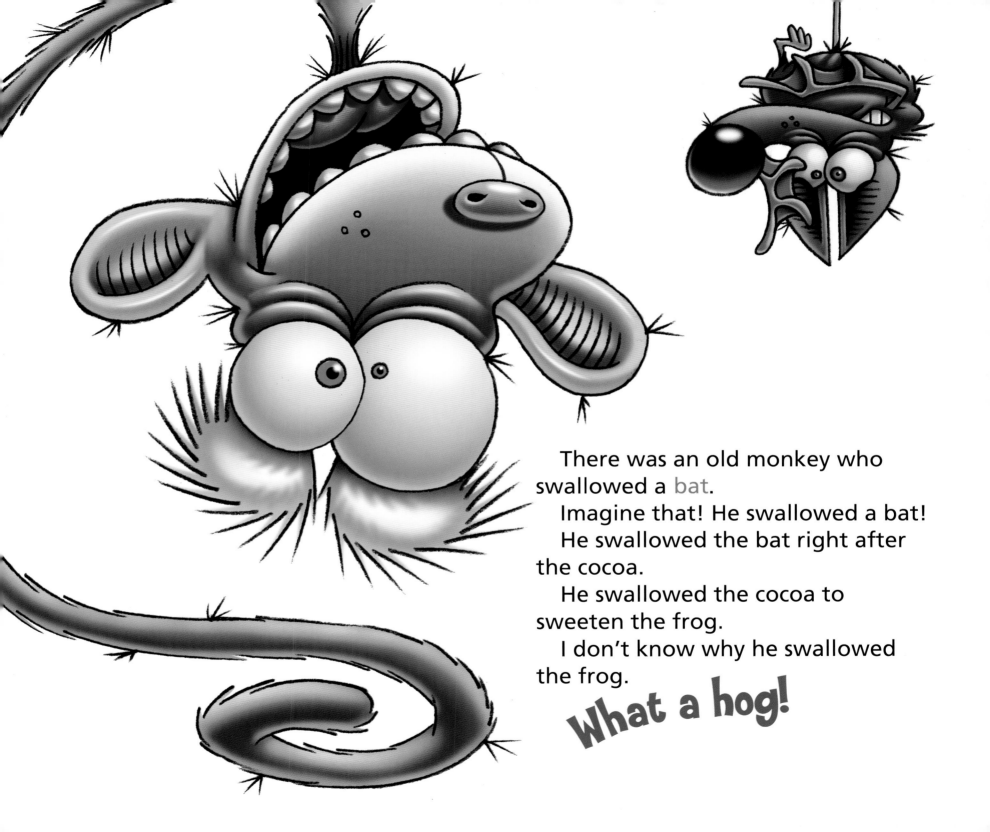

There was an old monkey who swallowed a bat.

Imagine that! He swallowed a bat!

He swallowed the bat right after the cocoa.

He swallowed the cocoa to sweeten the frog.

I don't know why he swallowed the frog.

What a hog!

There was an old monkey . . .

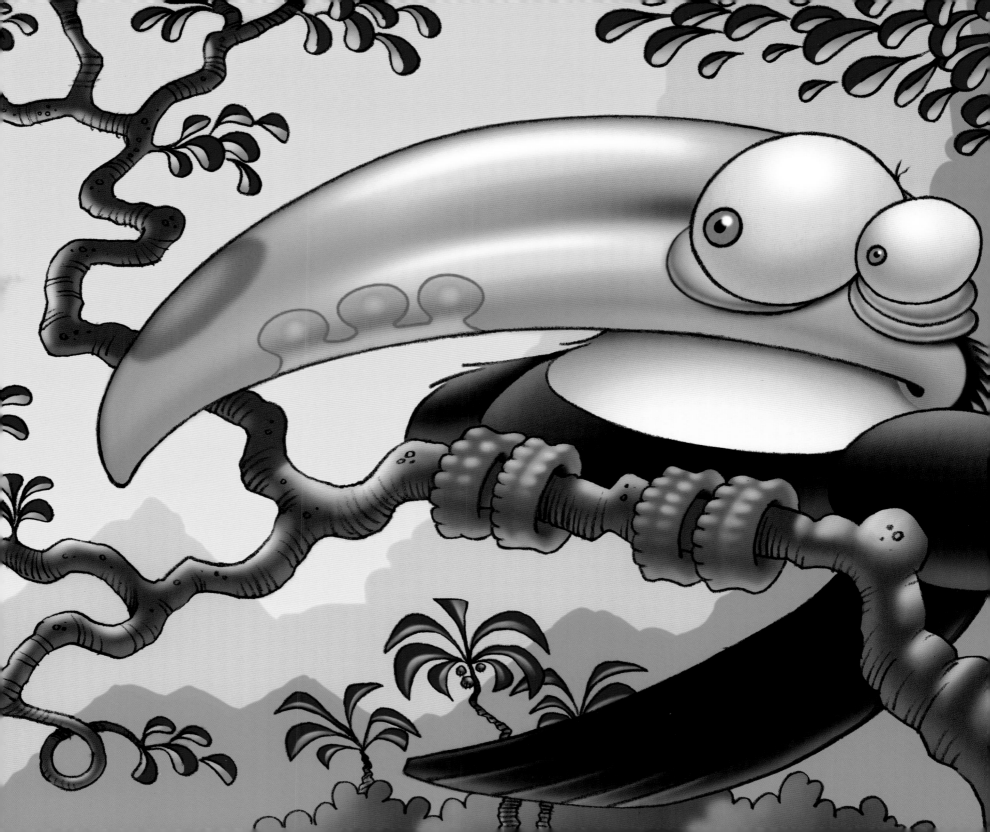

who swallowed **a** toucan.
I wouldn't try it, but certainly you can!

Hic!

He swallowed the toucan to squawk at the bat
He swallowed the bat right after the cocoa.
He swallowed the cocoa to sweeten the frog.
I don't know why he swallowed the frog.

What a hog!

There was an old monkey
who swallowed an iguana.
    I wouldn't eat it! But maybe
you'd wanna?

He swallowed the iguana to go with the toucan.
He swallowed the toucan to squawk at the bat.
He swallowed the bat right after the cocoa.
He swallowed the cocoa to sweeten the frog.
I don't know why he swallowed the frog.

What a hog!

There was an old monkey who swallowed a cat.
Gobbled it down, just like that!

He swallowed the cat to hunt the iguana.
He swallowed the iguana to go with the toucan.
He swallowed the toucan to squawk at the bat.
He swallowed the bat right after the cocoa.
He swallowed the cocoa to sweeten the frog.
I don't know why he swallowed the frog.

What a hog!

There was an old monkey
who swallowed a sloth.
He let out a cough when he
gulped down that sloth!

He swallowed the sloth to squash the cat.
He swallowed the cat to hunt the iguana.
He swallowed the iguana to go with the toucan.
He swallowed the toucan to squawk at the bat.
He swallowed the bat right after the cocoa.
He swallowed the cocoa to sweeten the frog.
I don't know why he swallowed the frog.

What a hog!

There was an old monkey who swallowed a tapir.
It tasted like paper, that rainforest tapir.

He swallowed the tapir to bump the sloth.
He swallowed the sloth to squash the cat.
He swallowed the cat to hunt the iguana.
He swallowed the iguana to go with the toucan.
He swallowed the toucan to squawk at the bat.
He swallowed the bat right after the cocoa.
He swallowed the cocoa to sweeten the frog.
I don't know why he swallowed the frog.

What a hog!

There was an old monkey who swallowed a mango.
He danced the tango while eating that mango!

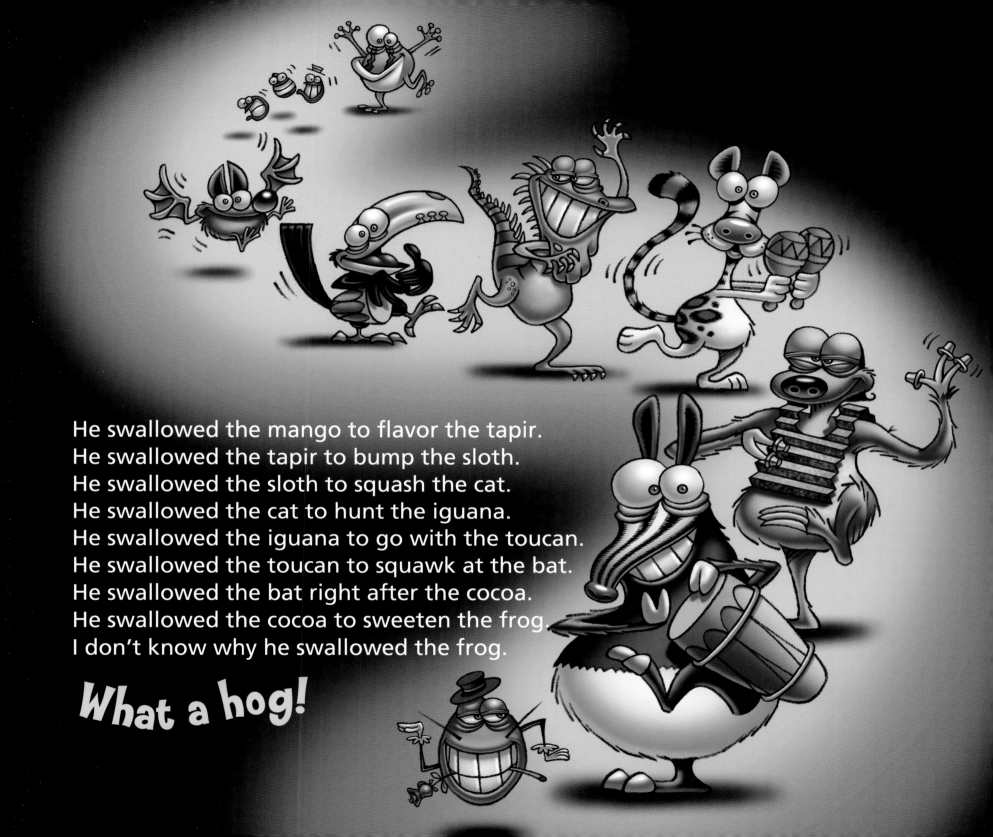

He swallowed the mango to flavor the tapir.
He swallowed the tapir to bump the sloth.
He swallowed the sloth to squash the cat.
He swallowed the cat to hunt the iguana.
He swallowed the iguana to go with the toucan.
He swallowed the toucan to squawk at the bat.
He swallowed the bat right after the cocoa.
He swallowed the cocoa to sweeten the frog.
I don't know why he swallowed the frog.

What a hog!

There was an old monkey
who swallowed a croc.
Plucked from a rock,
that sunny, old croc!

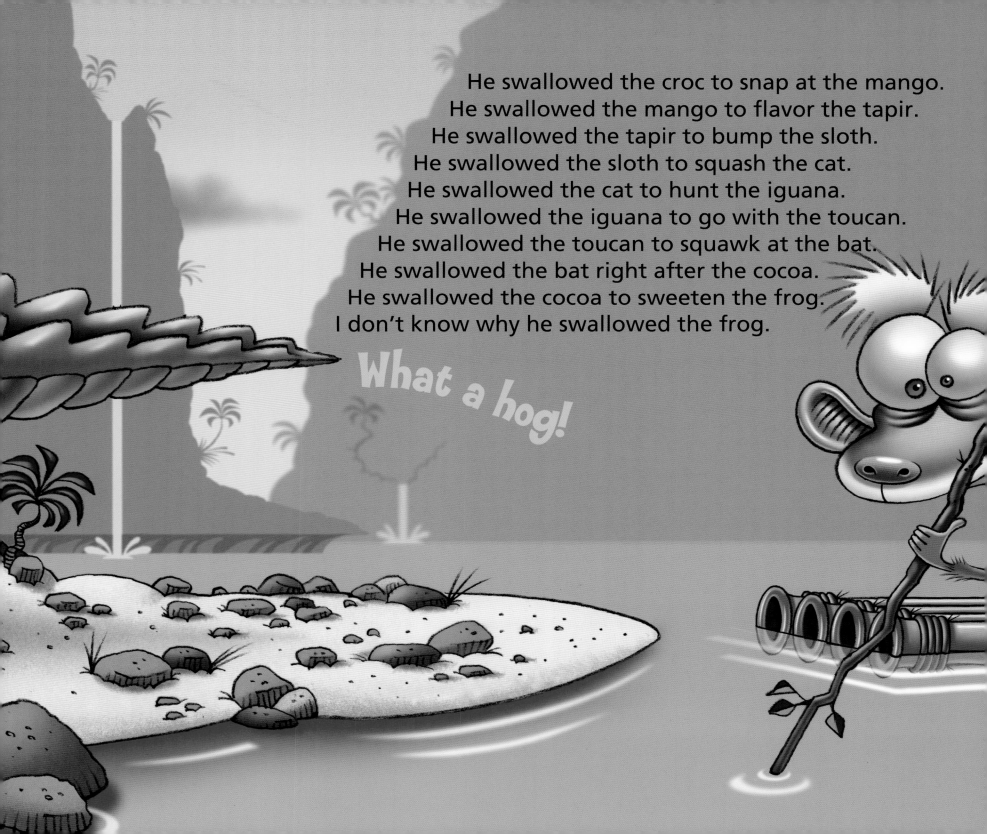

He swallowed the croc to snap at the mango.
He swallowed the mango to flavor the tapir.
He swallowed the tapir to bump the sloth.
He swallowed the sloth to squash the cat.
He swallowed the cat to hunt the iguana.
He swallowed the iguana to go with the toucan.
He swallowed the toucan to squawk at the bat.
He swallowed the bat right after the cocoa.
He swallowed the cocoa to sweeten the frog.
I don't know why he swallowed the frog.

What a hog!

There was an old monkey
who swallowed a vine.
  He slurped and he burped
as he dined on that vine.

He swallowed the vine to lasso the croc. He swallowed the croc to snap at the mango. He swallowed the mango to flavor the tapir. He swallowed the tapir to bump the sloth. He swallowed the sloth to squash the cat. He swallowed the cat to hunt the iguana. He swallowed the iguana to go with the toucan. He swallowed the toucan to squawk at the bat. He swallowed the bat right after the cocoa. He swallowed the cocoa to sweeten the frog. I don't know why he swallowed the frog.

What a hog!

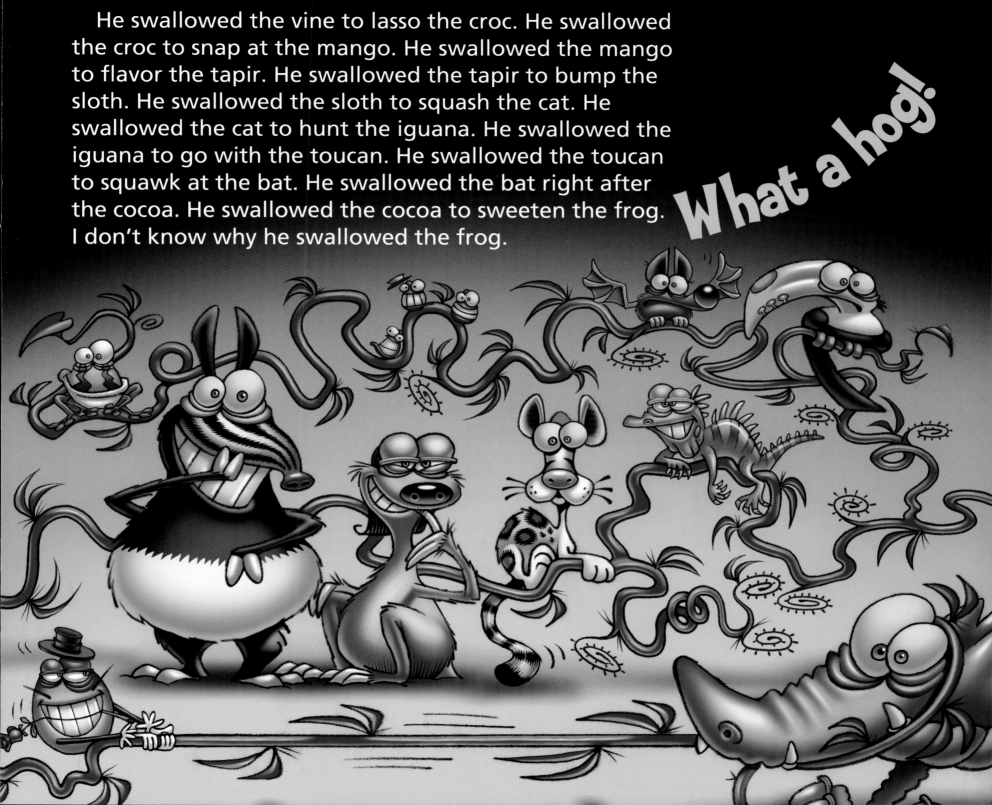

There was an old monkey
whose tummy did rumble.
Yours would, too . . .

if you swallowed a

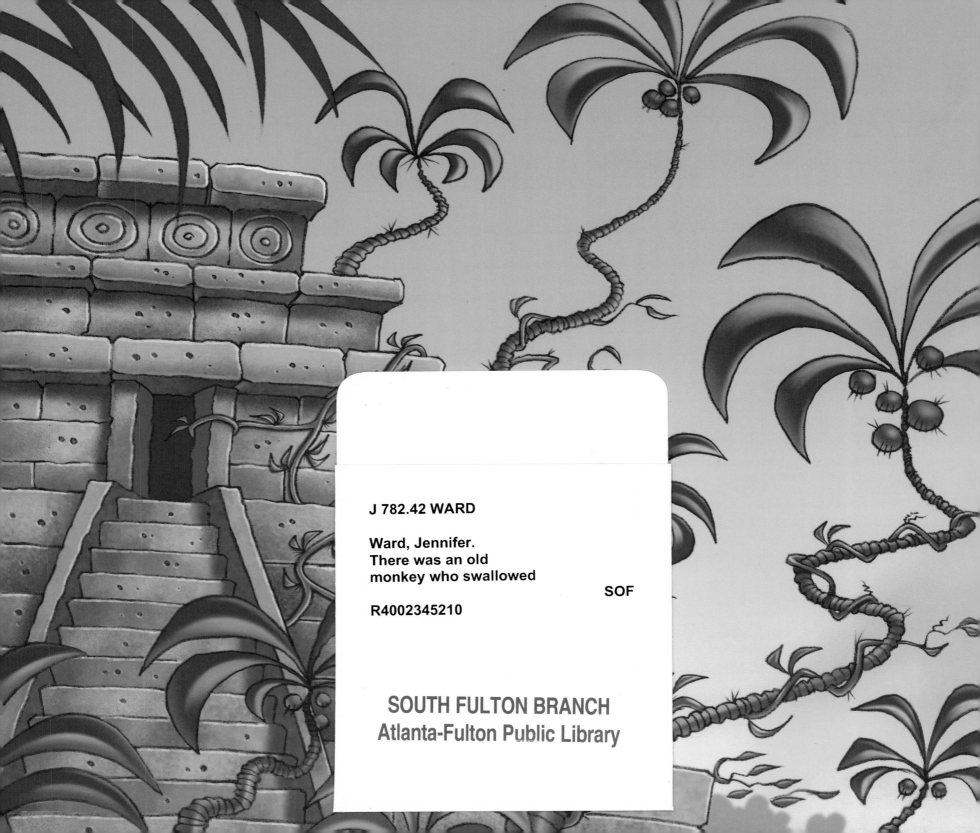